TRACTION MAN AND THE

BEACH ODYSSEY

MINI GREY

Alfred A. Knopf · New York

Everyone is going on holiday. Traction Man and his loyal pet, Scrubbing Brush, are doing an equipment check before they go.

underwater camera
cave helmet
safety vest
extra grip gloves
assorted harnesses
zip-up microsuit
aquatic air tanks
flexible flippers
high-energy rations

HOBBLE NOBBLES
ADVENTURE BISCUITS

ingeniously made of Potato
HOOPOS
wear them or eat them

GREAT SCOTT
EXPEDITION QUALITY
MINT CAKE
As used by
Captain Oatcake

INSTANT
JIFFY SOUP
CASSEROLE
FLAVOUR

BOXO
CUBE
JUST ADD WATER
FOR STOCK, SOUP,
STEW, BROTH, OR
A WARMING BREW

"All there?
Let's start loading, then."

Scrubbing Brush has never been on holiday before and is quite excited.

Granny's coming too. She has a new Young Pet called Truffles.

Scrubbing Brush thinks Truffles needs some Proper Training . . .

"My goodness! Look at that, Scrubbing Brush –
it must be the Wide Ocean!"

BIG AND SPARKLY

Traction Man and Scrubbing Brush are exploring the secret crevices of the Rockpool.

Traction Man is wearing his Squid-Proof Scuba Suit, Lightweight Shorts and Aquatic Air Tanks.

Who knows what creatures lurk in this Underwater World?

If they stay very still, perhaps some of the elusive Rockpool Animals will appear.

"Here, young Prawn, don't be shy!"

"I'd leave that well alone if I were you, Scrubbing Brush . . ."

"Oh dear – too late."

LUNCHTIME!

Nearly everyone wanted to have a quick dip in the sea before lunch –

which leaves Traction Man and Scrubbing Brush and . . .

OPERATION PICNIC.

"At all costs, this picnic must be defended against hungry Truffles."

DIG DIG DIG

But Truffles must think
Traction Man is some sort of bone
and has carried him off.

Oh no!
Traction Man is being
buried for later.

Don't worry, Traction Man, Scrubbing Brush has
sturdy bristles and will dig you out in a jiffy.

Scrubbing Brush is doing
a Victory Dance.

"Watch out behind you, Scrubbing Brush –
never leave your back to the sea!"

A huge seaweed mass
on a giant wave
swamps Scrubbing Brush
and carries him
away.

Arf!

Traction Man
just manages to grab
on to the seaweed.

Traction Man and Scrubbing Brush
are clinging on to a plastic bottle
in the vast sea.
They can hardly see land.

A colossal wave
towers
over them.

Traction Man is wearing
quite a lot of seaweed.

It's all dark.

"Scrubbing Brush,
where are you?"

Arf!

"Thank
goodness!"

"Can you see that shape
in the gloom?

Keep very still, Scrubbing Brush,
and don't be scared
(even though it has
hot breath
and dripping jaws).

But do you hear a voice?"

What have you got there, Fluffy?

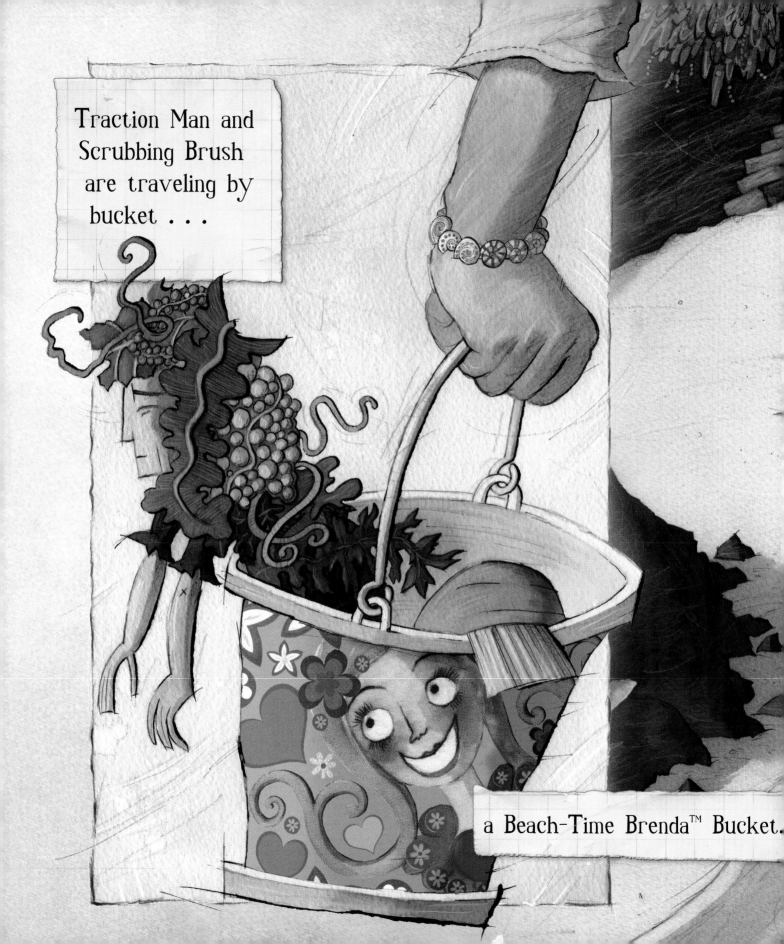

Traction Man and Scrubbing Brush are traveling by bucket . . .

a Beach-Time Brenda™ Bucket.

I don't see him anywhere, but
maybe he's been washed up
further along...

Traction Man is in the Dollies' Castle, wearing seaweed
hair and beard, a shell hat, a light dusting of sand
and a floral sarong.
Scrubbing Brush has been garlanded too.
The Dollies are treating them to a feast of
ice cream treats.

SNUFFLE SNUFFLE

"Look there, Scrubbing Brush –
do you recognize that nose?"

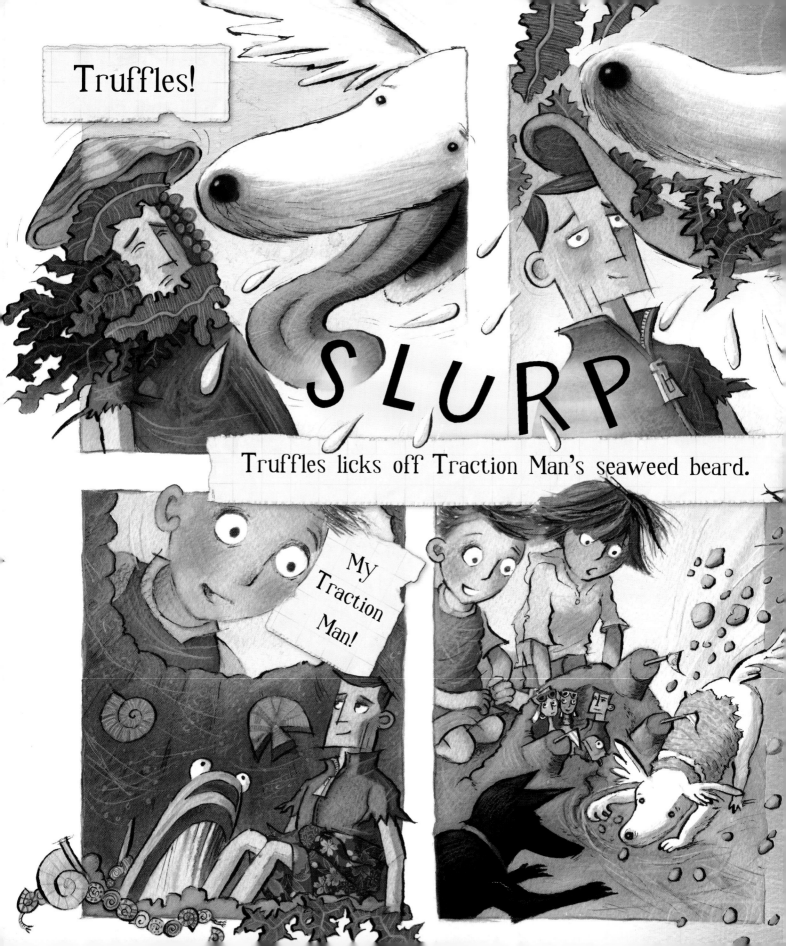

"No more time for ice cream, Ladies – Time for Action! There seems to be an earthquake going on in your castle. This structure is seriously unstable – it's crumbling everywhere."

"I'm afraid your castle has been demolished
by Truffles the Puppy.
But don't worry, Scrubbing Brush and I can
help you rebuild it in no time."

Traction Man, Scrubbing Brush and the Dollies
are digging an exploration hole
to the Center of the Earth.

(The Dollies are wearing Safety Jackets,
Excavation Shorts and Cave Helmets
borrowed from Traction Man.)

They have already unearthed
these buried treasures and the bones
of some ancient creature.

Behind them you can see
the Dollies' new castle.
They think it is Even Better than before.

Tomorrow they are all going to go
on an expedition to the Mysterious Cave
with their own lunch.

The Dollies have a dinghy . . .
and they are all
ready for
Anything.

Some other brilliant books by Mini Grey:

Egg Drop
The Very Smart Pea and the Princess-to-Be
Ginger Bear
Traction Man Is Here!
The Adventures of the Dish and the Spoon
Traction Man Meets Turbo Dog
Jim (by Hilaire Belloc, illustrated by Mini Grey)
Three by the Sea

THIS IS A BORZOI BOOK PUBLISHED BY ALFRED A. KNOPF

Copyright © 2011 by Mini Grey

All rights reserved. Published in hardcover in the United States by Alfred A. Knopf, an imprint of Random House Children's Books, a division of Random House, Inc., New York. Originally published in Great Britain by Jonathan Cape, an imprint of Random House Children's Books, a division of the Random House Group Ltd., London, in 2011.

Knopf, Borzoi Books, and the colophon are registered trademarks of Random House, Inc.

Visit us on the Web! randomhouse.com/kids

Educators and librarians, for a variety of teaching tools, visit us at randomhouse.com/teachers

Library of Congress Cataloging-in-Publication Data is available upon request.

ISBN 978-0-375-86952-5 (trade)   ISBN 978-0-375-96952-2 (lib. bdg.)

MANUFACTURED IN MALAYSIA

May 2012

10 9 8 7 6 5 4 3 2 1

First American Edition

Random House Children's Books supports the First Amendment and celebrates the right to read.

Dedicated to TIA